The Anger of Zeus

Mythology gives you interesting explanations about life and satisfies your curiosity with stories that have been made up to explain surprising or frightening phenomena.

People throughout the world have their own myths. In the imaginary world of mythology, humans can become birds or stars. The sun, wind, trees, and the rest of the natural world are full of gods who often interact with humans.

Greek and Roman mythology began more than 3,000 years ago. It consisted of stories first told by Greeks that lived on the shores of the Mediterranean Sea. In Italy the Romans would later borrow and modify many of these stories.

Most of the Greek myths were related to gods that resided upon the cloud-shrouded Mount Olympus. These clouds frequently could create a mysterious atmosphere on Mount Olympus. The ancient Greeks thought that their gods dwelt there and had human shapes, feelings, and behavior.

The Greeks and the Romans built temples, offered animal sacrifices, said prayers, performed plays, and competed in sports to please their humanlike gods on Mount Olympus.

How the world came into being in the first place?
Why is there night and day?
How did the four seasons come into existence?
Where do we go after we die?

Reading Greek and Roman mythology can help us understand the early human conceptions of the world. Since many Western ideas originated with the Greeks and Romans, you will benefit from taking a look into the mythology that helped to shape those ancient cultures. Understanding their mythology will give you an interesting view of the world you live in.

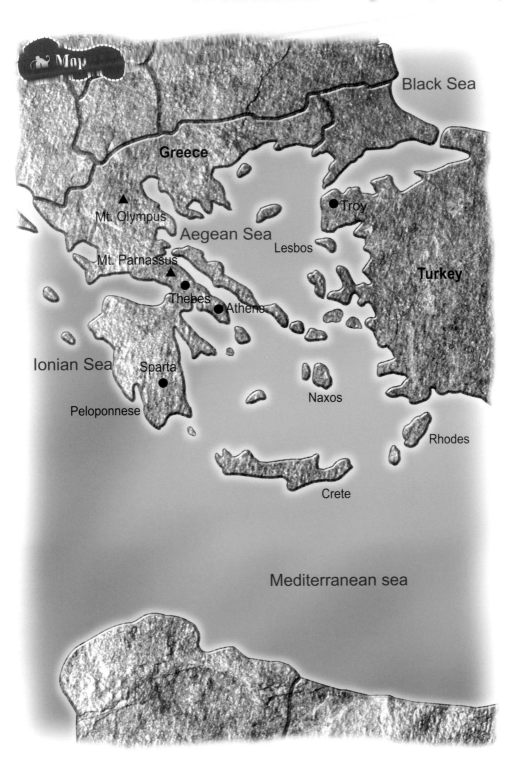

A long time ago, there were no humans in this world. Only gods existed. There were rivers, sea, mountains, valleys, and animals, but Zeus, king of gods felt something missing. Frustrated over this, Zeus decided to create humans shaped in the image of the gods. To perform a task that Zeus gave to create humans, Prometheus mixed a handful of earth with some water. That's how mankind first came into being. Unlike four-legged crawling animals, humans could walk upright on two legs, looking at the starts in the sky.

Prometheus wanted to give the best gifts to man, but due to a mistake of his brother, Epimetheus, Prometheus couldn't give any. So he stole fire for men, which was permitted only for gods. Fire gave man so many advantages in surviving; however, a terrible punishment was inflicted on Prometheus and humans: Prometheus had to be chained to a rock, while an eagle came to feast on his liver, and a flood completely destroyed mankind.

Thanks to the wisdom of his father, Prometheus, Deucalion and his wife survived the flood, becoming the new ancestor of mankind. This new civilization of human beings lived in harmony with each other and served gods well. Afterwards, a flood never occurred to destroy mankind.

The characters in the stories

Zeus
The king of gods

Poseidon
The king of the sea and water

Prometheus
One of Titans,
older brother of Epimetheus

Epimetheus
One of Titans,
younger brother
of Prometheus

Pandora
The first woman,
wife of Epimetheus

Deucalion
The son of Prometheus

Phyrra
The wife of Deucalion

Contents

Prometheus
and
Pandora

01

Long ago, there were rivers and valleys.

There were oceans and mountains.

There were birds, fish and animals.

But something was missing.

There were no men or women.

The earth was a very lonely place.

Zeus looked at the earth and was not happy.

"The earth is a beautiful place,
but it needs more.
We, the gods, will make a new animal.
He will be called man!"

"Hmm, what will man look like?
He must look different from the other animals.
Eureka! He will look like the gods of Olympus!"

Zeus called Prometheus and Epimetheus.

"You have a very important task," said Zeus,

"You will make a new animal called man.

Man will walk on two legs.

Animals look downward, toward the earth,

but man must be very different.

Yes, man will look upward, toward the stars."

Prometheus was a very wise Titan.

He could see the future.

At first, Zeus liked Prometheus.

Prometheus even fought beside Zeus

during The Battle of the Titans.

He always tried to help man.

 03

Epimetheus was Prometheus's brother.

He was a very stupid, silly Titan.

He often did silly things.

Sometimes, this caused big problems.

Prometheus and Epimetheus went away.

They had lots of work to do.

Prometheus told his brother what to do.

"Epimetheus, I will make man,

but you have a big job, too.

You will give different gifts to the animals.

But remember! Man must have the best gifts!"

Epimetheus began his job.

In a box, there were the gifts.

One by one, he gave the gifts to the animals.

"Let's see . . . I'll give courage to the tiger.

I'll give speed to the deer.

I'll give power to the bear.

I'll give smarts to the monkey."

Prometheus mixed the earth and water together.
Then he shaped the wet earth into man.
"Ah! Success!" said Prometheus.
Then Prometheus looked around at the animals.
It seemed that Epimetheus did a fine job.
"You did a good job. Now we must give
the gifts to man!" said Prometheus.

Epimetheus looked into the box.
Suddenly, he looked very worried.
"Uh, Prometheus," said Epimetheus,
"I guess I used all the good gifts.
There is only bad stuff left."
"What? Now what are we going to do?"
yelled Prometheus.
Prometheus thought hard.
Then he had an idea.
"I'll give fire to man. That's a great gift!"

Hephaestus was the god of fire.

Prometheus stole fire, and gave it to man.

With fire, man ruled all animals.

Now, man made weapons.

He made tools for farming.

He heated his home.

Fire really was the greatest gift of all.

But Zeus found out
about the gift.
He was very angry.
He met with the other gods
and goddesses.
"Prometheus gave fire to man!"
yelled Zeus,
"But fire was only for the gods!
We must punish Prometheus.
But first, we will punish man!"

Zeus told Hephaestus to make woman.

Her name was Pandora.

Then the gods of Olympus gave gifts to her.

First, Aphrodite gave her beauty.

Then, Athena taught her how to make cloth.

Next,

Apollo taught her how to sing and play music.

But Hermes taught her how to lie.

Pandora

Then Zeus gave Pandora to Epimetheus.

"Congratulations! You did a fine job.

Please take this gift.

Her name is Pandora.

She is now yours."

"Gosh, Zeus! She's beautiful," said Epimetheus,

"Thank you so much. I really like her!

Come on, Pandora. Let's go meet my brother."

"Look, Prometheus! Look what Zeus gave me!"

"Hmm, You'd better be careful.

Zeus can be very tricky!" said Prometheus.

"But look at her. She's beautiful," said Epimetheus,

"I'm sure she won't make any trouble. I'm sure!"

There was a box on a table in Epimetheus's
house. It was filled with bad things.
"Epimetheus," asked Pandora,
"What's in the box?"
"Oh, it's filled with bad things."
said Epimetheus,
"Don't open it! Never open the box!
Don't even look at it!"

But Pandora could not forget the box.

She opened the box.

Suddenly all the bad things came out.

Sickness, sadness and anger came out.

Fighting and war came out.

goodness

fighting

war

Hope

26

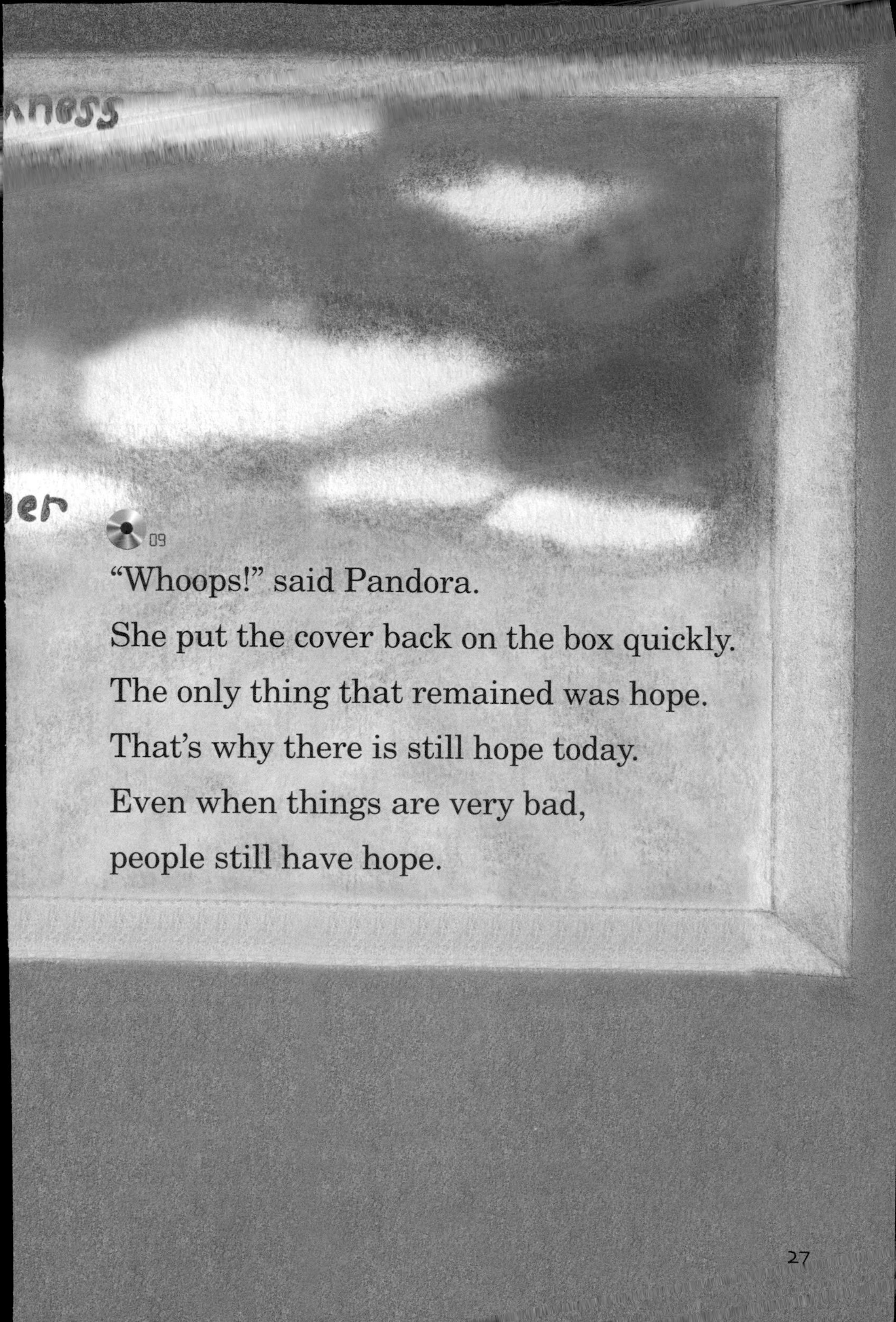

er

09

"Whoops!" said Pandora.

She put the cover back on the box quickly.

The only thing that remained was hope.

That's why there is still hope today.

Even when things are very bad,

people still have hope.

For stealing fire,
Zeus punished Prometheus.
He tied Prometheus to a stake.
Then, every morning an eagle tore out his liver.
In the evening the liver grew back.
This happened each day for thirty years.
Finally, Hercules felt sorry for him.
He killed the eagle and freed Prometheus.

Deucalion's Flood

After Pandora opened the box,
the world became a terrible place.
Truth and honor went away.
Crime was a big problem.
Man fought long, deadly wars.

Everyone was greedy.

Everyone lied.

Sons killed their own fathers.

Man was killing himself.

And he was killing the earth, too.

Zeus was very angry.

He called a meeting of all the gods.

Gods came from all over the universe.

"The earth is bad because of man.

Man has become wicked and evil.

I will cause a great flood and kill all men.

After man is gone, we will begin again."

Prometheus was afraid at Zeus's words.
Prometheus had a son named Deucalion.
His son was a man, not a god,
but his son was a good, honest man.
His son didn't cause any problems.
Prometheus didn't want his son to die.
After the meeting,
he went down to the earth quickly.

"Son, there is no time to waste!" said Prometheus,

"Zeus is going to cause a big flood.

He is going to kill all men.

You must build a big boat.

Put all the things you'll need on the boat.

Put animals, food and tools on the boat.

You will be safe on the boat."

Deucalion and his wife, Phyrra, worked hard.

They worked day and night on the boat.

In just one week, they finished it.

Then, they put animals, food and tools on the boat.

It began to rain. Then, it began to pour.

There was bright lightning and loud thunder.

The water covered houses and temples.

But Zeus was not satisfied.

"Poseidon, I need your help," said Zeus,

"You are the god of the sea and water.

Use your mighty power.

There must be no dry land on the earth!"

Then Poseidon hit the water with his **spear**.

Giant waves came up.

Soon, even the mountains were covered.

But on the boat, Deucalion and Phyrra were safe.

The animals and food were safe, too.

For nine days, the terrible storm continued.

Both Phyrra and Deucalion were scared.

They thought the storm wouldn't stop.

Deucalion and Phyrra prayed to Zeus.

They asked Zeus to stop the storm.

Poseidon

Zeus heard their prayers.

He knew that Deucalion and Phyrra were good people

He also knew no other people were alive.

Everyone else was dead.

Zeus felt sorry for Deucalion and his wife.

So he stopped the rain.

The sky was blue at last.

But there was water everywhere.

For days, Deucalion's big boat floated on the water.

And each day, he and his wife prayed to Zeus.

Finally, the water started to go down.

The big boat sat on Mount Parnassus.

Deucalion and his wife opened the doors.

They let all the animals free.

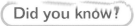

Mount Parnassus

Mount Parnassus is next to the town of Delphi.

Apollo killed a scary, huge snake on this mountain.

In old Greece,

there were special sports events here.

These events made people remember

how Apollo killed the snake.

Near the town, there is a famous temple.

The temple is for the god Apollo.

The Temple of Apollo

Then Deucalion and Phyrra went to a temple.
The temple was in bad condition because of
the water. They lit a fire. Then they prayed.
First, they thanked Zeus, king of the gods.
Then Deucalion said, "We are alone.
There are no other people on the earth.
The earth must have more people. Help us, Zeus."

Again, Zeus heard Deucalion's prayers.

He said, "Leave the temple. When you get outside, throw down your mother's bones on the ground!"

Phyrra was shocked.

"I can't throw my mother's bones on the ground!"

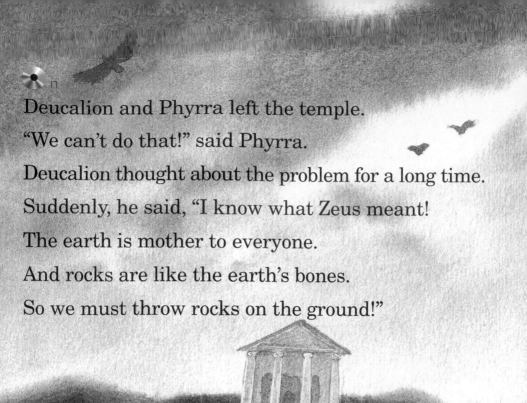

Deucalion and Phyrra left the temple.

"We can't do that!" said Phyrra.

Deucalion thought about the problem for a long time.

Suddenly, he said, "I know what Zeus meant!

The earth is mother to everyone.

And rocks are like the earth's bones.

So we must throw rocks on the ground!"

They picked up many rocks.

They walked around the temple.

They threw down hundreds of rocks.

Then they turned around and looked.

They were surprised.

Deucalion and Phyrra

 18

The rocks were slowly getting soft.

Then they wiggled and shook.

They started to look like people.

The rocks did change into people.

Deucalion's rocks changed into men.

Phyrra's rocks changed into women.

The new people weren't as good as before,

but they tried to do well and were hard workers.

Zeus looked down on them from Mount Olympus.

The new people tried hard.

The new people helped each other.

Soon, truth and honor came back.

Also, the new people prayed to the gods.

This made him very happy.

And Zeus never flooded the world again.

Noah's Ark

The bible also has a similar story

to the Deucalion's Flood.

In this story,

God saw many bad people on the earth.

So he decided to cover the earth with water.

But then God remembered Noah.

Noah and his family were the only good people.

So seven days before 'The Flood,'

God told Noah to make a huge boat.

This boat was called 'Noah's Ark.'

Noah built the ark for his family

and one pair of each animal.

It rained for forty days.

But Noah's family and the animals were safe in the

ark.

Reading Comprehension

Part 1

Prometheus and Pandora

🌙 Read the questions and choose
the best answers.

1. Who is Prometheus's stupid brother?
   (A) Epimetheus   (B) Poseidon
   (C) Zeus   (D) Hephaestus

2. Who stole fire?
   (A) Epimetheus   (B) Prometheus
   (C) Man   (D) Hephaestus

3. Prometheus was _____.
   (A) a god   (B) a man
   (C) a Titan   (D) an animal

4. Who taught Pandora to lie?
   (A) Hercules （B) Athena
   (C) Hermes （D) Apollo

5. Write the correct answer in the empty space.
   Animals look downward, toward the _____.

   Man will look upward, toward the _____.

6. Who freed Prometheus?
   (A) Epimetheus （B) Hera
   (C) Zeus （D) Hercules

7. To make man, what did Prometheus mix with water?
   (A) air （B) earth
   (C) light （D) salt

8. What didn't come out of Pandora's box?
   (A) war （B) sickness
   (C) hope （D) fighting

Part 2
Deucalion's Flood

🎵 Read the questions and choose
   the best answers.

1. Who is Deucalion?

   (A) Epimetheus's son   (B) Prometheus's son

   (C) Hera's son   (D) Phyrra's son

2. Who is Deucalion's wife?

   (A) Pandora   (B) Athena

   (C) Hera   (D) Phyrra

3. Who helped Zeus flood the world?

   (A) Deucalion   (B) Poseidon

   (C) Hades   (D) Apollo

4. How long did the rain come down?

    (A) for seven days   (B) for eight days

    (C) for nine days   (D) for ten days

5. What did Zeus mean by 'mother's bones'?

    (A) air   (B) earth

    (C) water   (D) rocks

6. Write the correct answer in the empty space.

    Deucalion's rocks changed into _____.

    Phyrra's rocks changed into _____.

7. What didn't make Zeus angry?

    (A) Men fought long, deadly wars.

    (B) Everyone lied.

    (C) Man was killing the earth.

    (D) Man prayed to the gods.

希臘羅馬神話故事 ❸

宙斯之怒 The Anger of Zeus

First Published March, 2011
First Printing March, 2011

Original Story by Thomas Bulfinch
Rewritten by Jeff Zeter
Illustrated by Koltsova Irina
Designer: Eonju No
Translated by Jia-chen Chuo

Printed and distributed by Cosmos Culture Ltd.
Tel: 02-2365-9739
Fax: 02-2365-9835
http://www.icosmos.com.tw
Publisher: Value-Deliver Culture Ltd.

Pandora

The Anger of Zeus

中譯解答本

卓加真　譯

歡迎來到神話的世界

　　神話用有趣的方式說明生命，各種故事解釋各種奇異或可怕現象，滿足人們的好奇心。世界上的每個民族，都有自己的神話。在神話的奇幻世界裡，人類可以化身成鳥或星辰。太陽、風、樹木等等，自然界萬物皆充滿了和人類互動頻繁的神靈。

　　希臘和羅馬神話的出現，已超過三千年，源自居住在地中海岸的希臘人。之後，再由義大利的羅馬人所接受，並進一步改寫之。

　　希臘神話的故事，大都與雲霄上的奧林帕斯山諸神有關。雲霧常為奧林帕斯山蒙上神祕的氣氛，古希臘人認為，神明就住在山上，其形體、感情和行為舉止，無異於人。希臘人和羅馬人建立寺廟、獻祭動物、祈禳，並用戲劇和運動競賽的方式，來取悅那些住在奧林帕斯山、與人同形同性的眾神。

　　世界最初是如何形成的？
　　為什麼會有晝夜之分？
　　為什麼會有四季變化？
　　人死後將從何而去？

　　閱讀希臘羅馬神話，可以幫助我們瞭解早期人類的世界觀。又因許多西方思想乃源自於希臘人和羅馬人，故窺視希臘羅馬神話，將有助於塑造出那些古文化的真貌。瞭解這些神話的內容，將可以讓人們對這個世界別有一番趣解。

　　很久以前，世界上還沒有人類，只有神明。當時的世界雖然有河流、海洋、山脈、溪谷和動物，但眾神之王宙斯卻仍覺得少了些什麼。有感於此，宙斯決定要用神的形象創造出人類。

　　為了要執行宙斯這項「創造人類」的任務，普羅米修斯用水和了一把泥土，那正是人類一開始的雛型。和四足動物不同的是，人類可以用兩腿直立走路，並抬頭仰望天上的星辰。

　　普羅米修斯原本是想把最好的禮物賜給人類，但由於弟弟伊比米修斯的一個過失，普羅米修斯沒有禮物可贈予人類。於是，他便將只准許神明所使用的「火」，盜去送給人類使用。

　　火，帶給人們生活上的許多好處，但普羅米修斯和人類也為此付出了可怕的代價。普羅米修斯被鎖鏈牢牢地拴在石頭上，在老鷹啄食他的肝臟的同時，一場大洪水毀滅了人類。

　　拜父親普羅米修斯的智慧，鐸卡連和妻子逃過了洪水一劫，成為了人類的新始祖。這個新的人類文明，彼此和睦相處，對神明心存虔敬。從此，就再沒有大洪水來毀滅人類了。

目錄

普羅米修斯和潘朵拉

很久很久以前，
世界上有河川、山谷，
有海洋和山脈，
有群鳥、魚隻和動物，
卻獨獨少了男人和女人。
大地一片孤寂。
宙斯望著大地，
心中悶悶不樂。

- **long ago** [lɑːŋ əˋgoʊ]
  許久以前
- **valley** [ˋvælɪ] 山谷；溪谷
- **ocean** [ˋoʊʃən]
  海洋；大海
- **something** [ˋsʌmθɪŋ]
  某種事物
- **miss** [mɪs]
  遺漏；未達到
- **men** [mæn] 人類；男人
  （man的複數）
- **women** [ˋwɪmɪn] 女人
  （woman的複數）
- **lonely** [ˋloʊnlɪ]
  孤獨的；荒涼的
- **earth** [ɜːθ] 大地

「大地是個美麗的地方。
但卻缺少了什麼。
諸神要創造新的動物，
稱為人類！」

- **need** [niːd] 需要
- **god** [gɑːd] 神
- **make** [meɪk]
  創造；製造
- **look like** [lʊk laɪk]
  看起來像

「人類該長得什麼樣子呢？
他們的外表，
一定要和其他的動物不一樣。
有了！
他們要長得和奧林帕斯山上的神祇一樣！」

- **different from**
  [ˈdɪfənt frɑ:m]
  不同於……
- **the other** [ði: `ʌðə]
  其他的；另外的
- **Eureka** [juəˋri:kə]
  有了！；我知道了！
  （感嘆詞，現用以表示重大發現和解決困難後的喜悅）
- **Olympus** [oˋlɪmpəs]
  奧林帕斯仙境

---

p. 12

宙斯召喚普羅米修斯和伊比米修斯。
宙斯說：
「你們有項重要任務，
要負責創造新的動物，名為人類。
人類要以兩隻腳走路，
動物是兩眼朝下，看著地上，
但人類不一樣，
人類要兩眼朝上，仰望群星。」

- **important** [ɪmˋpɔ:rtn̩t]
  重大；重要的
- **task** [tæsk] 任務
- **walk** [wɑ:k]
  走路；行走
- **downward** [ˋdaun.wəd]
  向下地
- **toward** [tuˋwɔ:rd]
  向；朝
- **different** [ˋdɪfənt]
  不同的；不一樣的
- **upward** [ˋʌpwəd]
  向上地
- **star** [stɑ:r] 星星；恒星

普羅米修斯是位聰明的泰坦神，
他可以預知未來。
宙斯最初是很尊敬他的，
他曾與宙斯並肩作戰，
對抗其他的泰坦神，
而普羅米修斯也盡量對人類伸出援手。

- **wise** [waɪz]
  聰明的；有智慧的
- **Titan** [ˋtaɪtən]
  泰坦神族
- **future** [ˋfju:tʃə] 未來
- **at first** [æt ˋfɜ:st]
  最初；開始時
- **even** [ˋi:vən]
  更確切地說
- **fought** [fɑ:t] 作戰；戰鬥
  (fight的過去式)
- **during** [ˋdʊrɪŋ]
  在某段時間中
- **battle** [ˋbætḷ] 戰爭
- **always** [ˋɑ:lweɪz]
  總是；無論什麼時候

伊比米修斯是普羅米修斯的胞弟，
但他是個愚昧無知的泰坦神。
他常做出愚蠢可笑的事情，
有時還會闖禍。

- **brother** [ˋbrʌðə] 兄弟
- **stupid** [ˋstju:pɪd]
  愚蠢的
- **silly** [ˋsɪli]
  呆傻的；無意義的
- **sometimes** [ˋsʌmtaɪmz]
  有時候；偶爾
- **cause** [kɑ:z]
  導致；引起
- **problem** [ˋprɑ:.bləm]
  問題

p. 15

他們兩人向宙斯告退，
還有繁重的工作等著他們去完成。
哥哥交代弟弟他的工作內容：
「伊比米修斯，我要創造人類，
但你也有個重要任務。
你要負責賜給動物各種天賦，
但別忘了，要將最好的留給人類！」

- **went away** [went ə`meɪ]
  離開；離家
- **lots of** [lɑ:ts ɑ:v] 許多
- **what to do**
  [wɑ:t tə du:] 該做什麼
- **gift** [gɪft] 天賦；天資
- **remember** [rɪ`membə]
  記得

---

p. 16

伊比米修斯於是開始實行任務。
所有的天賦，都裝在一個盒子裡，
他把裡頭的天賦一個個給了動物。
「讓我看看嘛，
我將勇氣賜給老虎。
將速度賜給鹿兒。
將力氣賜給熊隻。
將機智賜給猴子。」

- **began** [bɪ`gæn]
  開始著手；進行
  （begin的過去式）
- **one by one**
  [wʌn baɪ wʌn]
  一個接著一個
- **courage** [`kɜ:rɪdʒ]
  勇氣
- **speed** [spi:d] 速度
- **power** [pauə] 力量
- **smarts** [smɑ:rts]
  機靈；機智

---

p. 17

普羅米修斯將泥土和水混合，
然後用泥巴塑造成人類。
「完成了！」普羅米修斯說道。
普羅米修斯看看周圍的動物，

- **mix** [mɪks] 混合
- **shape A into B**
  [ʃeɪp eɪ `ɪntu: bi:]
  將A製作成B
- **wet** [wet] 濕的

7

看來，伊比米修斯做得很稱職。
「你做得不錯。
現在，我們將天賦賜給人類吧！」
普羅米修斯說。

- **success** [səkˋses] 成功
- **look around**
  [lʊk əˋraʊnd] 環顧
- **seem** [si:m] 似乎；好像

----

p. 18

伊比米修斯看著盒內，
神情突然慌張了起來。
他說道：「啊，哥哥，
恐怕所有天賦都用光了，
只剩下壞的東西了。」
哥哥叫道：「什麼？那怎麼辦？」
普羅米修斯想了又想，
終於有了一個主意。
「我要將火種賜給人類，
這是個很不錯的禮物！」

- **suddenly** [ˋsʌdənʒli]
  突然地
- **worried** [ˋwʌrid]
  有煩惱的
- **guess** [ges] 推測；猜想
- **only** [ˋəʊnli]
  唯一的；僅有的
- **stuff** [stʌf]
  （泛指）東西；事物
- **yell** [jell] 大聲喊叫
- **hard** [hɑ:rd]
  拼命地；努力地

----

p. 19

赫發斯特斯是火神。
普羅米修斯卻偷了火種，
送給了人類。
人類靠著火，統管所有動物，
而且還製造武器，
並利用工具耕作。

- **stole** [stəʊl]
  偷；盜（steal的過去式）
- **rule** [ru:l] 支配；統治
- **weapon** [ˋwepən]
  武器；兵器
- **tool** [tu:l] 工具
- **farming** [ˋfɑ:rmɪŋ]
  農業的

人類家中有了火的溫暖。
的確，火是最殊勝的禮物了。

- **heat** [hiːt] 使暖和
- **greatest** [ˋgretɪst] 最好的；最棒的

---

 p. 20

宙斯發現此事之後，大發雷霆。
他找其他眾神商量，
吼道：「普羅米修斯將火種給了人類！
火是神的專屬之物呀！
我們要懲罰普羅米修斯。
但在此之前，
我們先要懲罰人類！」

- **found out** [faʊnd aʊt] 發現（find out的過去式）
- **angry** [ˋæŋgri] 氣憤；發怒
- **goddess** [ˋgɑːdes] 女神
- **punish** [ˋpʌnɪʃ] 懲罰

---

 p. 21

宙斯先要火神創造女人，
命名為潘朵拉。
然後，
再由奧林帕斯山上的諸神贈饋她禮物。
首先，阿芙柔黛蒂送她美貌；
接著，雅典娜教她織布；
阿波羅教她歌唱、彈奏樂器；
而荷米斯，卻教她說謊。

- **beauty** [ˋbjuːᴛi] 美貌
- **taught** [tɑːt] 教導（teach的過去式）
- **how to** [haʊ tə] 如何；怎麼
- **cloth** [klɑːθ] 布；織物
- **lie** [laɪ] 說謊

9

宙斯將潘朵拉送予伊比米修斯。
「恭喜呀！你做得不錯。
請接受這個禮物，她名叫潘朵拉，
她現在是屬於你的了。」
伊比米修斯說道：
「天啊，宙斯，她真美。
感謝您的賜禮，我很喜歡她。
來吧，潘朵拉，
我們一起去見見我的兄弟吧。」

- **congratulations**
  [kɑnˌɡrætjuˋleʃənz]
  恭禧
- **take** [teɪk]
  收下；接受
- **come on** [kʌm ɑːn]
  來吧（表示懇求）

「看呀，普羅米修斯！
你看看宙斯賜給我的禮物！」
普羅米修斯說：
「你最好小心，
宙斯很老奸巨猾！」。
伊比米修斯回答：
「可是你看看她，她這麼美，
我想她一定不會惹禍的，
一定不會的！」

- **had better** [həd ˋbɛt̬.ə]
  最好；應該還是……
- **careful** [ˋkɛrʒfəl]
  小心的；當心的
  （careless粗心的）
- **tricky** [ˋtrɪki]
  狡猾的；奸詐的
- **won't** [woʊnt] 將不會
  （will not的縮寫）
- **trouble** [ˋtrʌbl] 麻煩
- **make trouble**
  [meɪk ˋtrʌbl] 惹麻煩

p. 24

伊比米修斯的桌子上有一個盒子，
盒中裝滿罪惡。
潘朵拉問道：「伊比米修斯呀，
盒子裡頭裝的是什麼東西啊？」
伊比米修斯回答：
「都是裝些邪惡的東西，
妳千萬不可以把盒子打開，
甚至連瞧都不要去瞧它！」

- **be filled with**
  [bi: fɪld wɪð]
  裝滿；使充滿
- **never** [ˋnevɚ] 絕不能
- **look at** [lʊk æt] 看；盯

p. 25

然而，潘朵拉對盒子念念不忘，
就把它給打開了。
頃刻間，所有的罪惡傾巢而出，
疾病，哀愁，憤怒，
從盒子裡跑了出來，
鬥爭，戰爭，也跑了出來。

- **forget** [fɚˋget]
  忘懷；忘掉
- **came out** [keɪm aʊt]
  跑出來
  （come out的過去式）
- **sickness** [ˋsɪknəs] 疾病
- **sadness** [ˋsædnəs]
  悲傷；憂愁
- **anger** [ˋæŋɡɚ] 憤怒
- **fighting** [faɪtɪŋ] 打鬥
- **war** [wɔ:r] 戰爭

p. 27

「哎呀！」潘朵拉叫道。
她連忙將盒子蓋上，
唯一還留在盒子裡的是希望。
也因此，時至今日，

- **whoops** [wu:ps]
  哎呀；哎喲
- **put back** [pʊt bæk]
  放回原處
- **cover** [ˋkʌvɚ] 蓋子

人間還擁有希望。
儘管遭遇困厄,
人仍會心存希望。

* **quickly** [ˋkwɪk.li]
  快速地
* **remain** [rɪˋmeɪn]
  保持不變
* **hope** [hoʊp] 希望
* **still** [stɪl] 仍然

---

p. 28

宙斯為偷火一事,
懲罰普羅米修斯。
他將普羅米修斯綁在樁上,
每天早上,
會有一隻老鷹啄出他的肝臟,
到了晚上,肝臟又會長回來。
三十年來,如此日復一日。
最後,大力士赫丘力很不忍心,
便殺了老鷹,
釋放了普羅米修斯。

* **tie** [taɪ] 捆綁
* **stake** [steɪk] 樁
* **eagle** [ˋi:.gl] 老鷹
* **tore out** [tɔ:r aʊt]
  撕咬;扯出
  (tear out的過去式)
* **liver** [ˋlɪvə] 肝臟
* **grew back** [gru: bæk]
  重新長出
  (grow back的過去式)
* **each day** [i:tʃ deɪ]
  每一天
* **felt sorry for** [felt ˋsɔ:ri]
  為⋯⋯感到可憐
  (feel sorry的過去式)
* **free** [fri:] 釋放;使自由

鐸卡連的洪水

自從潘朵拉打開了盒子之後，
人間變成了一座煉獄。
真理和榮譽蕩然無存，
罪惡到處可見。
人類長期戰亂，死傷無數。

- **terrible** [`ter.ə.bl̩]
  可怕的；駭人的
- **truth** [tru:θ]
  真理；真實
- **honor** [`ɑ:nɚ] 榮譽
- **crime** [kraɪm] 犯罪
- **deadly** [`ded.li] 致命地

人心貪婪，謊言遍布。
子弒父，人們自相殘殺，
也戕害了大地。

- **greedy** [`gri:.di] 貪婪
- **own** [oʊn]
  嫡親的；自己的
  （表示血緣關係）
- **himself** [hɪm`self]
  他自己

宙斯為此震怒不已。
他召來眾神共議，
眾神從宇宙各地趕來。
「人類破壞大地，
邪惡無比。
我要製造大洪水，
毀滅人類。

- **meeting** [mi:tɪŋ] 集會
- **universe** [`ju:.nɪ.vɜ:s]
  宇宙
- **because of** [bɪ`kɑ:z ɑ:v]
  因為；由於
- **wicked** [`wɪkɪd]
  邪惡的
- **evil** [`i:.vəl]
  壞的；懷惡意的

13

等人類滅亡之後，
我們再重新開始。」

- **flood** [flʌd] 洪水；水災
- **gone** [gɑ:n] 消失
  （go的過去分詞）
- **begin** [bɪˋgɪn] 開始

---

p. 33

宙斯的話，
讓普羅米修斯聽得憂心忡忡。
普羅米修斯有一個叫做鐸卡連的兒子，
鐸卡連是一個凡人，
爲人善良誠實，未曾闖過禍。
普羅米修斯不希望兒子喪命，
他在眾神會議之後，便連忙下到凡間。

- **afraid** [əˋfreɪd]
  害怕的；恐懼的
- **word** [wɜ:d] 話語
- **honest** [ˋɑ:.nɪst]
  誠實的

---

p. 34

普羅米修斯說：
「兒子，時間緊迫！
宙斯準備製造大洪水，
他打算消滅人類。
你趕快去建造一艘巨船，
把所有你需要的東西都安置到船上去，
動物、食物、工具，都帶上船。
待在船上，就可以安然無事了。」

- **waste** [weɪst] 浪費
- **be going to** [bi: gouɪŋ tə]
  即將要
- **build** [bɪld] 建造；修建
- **put** [put] 放；置
- **safe** [seɪf] 安全

14

p. 35

鐸卡連和妻子皮雅努力造船，
日以繼夜地趕工。
一星期後，船便大工告成。
接著，
他們將動物、食物和工具都帶上船。
這時，天空開始下起雨來，
繼之傾盆大雨，雷電交加。
洪水淹沒了房屋和寺廟。

- **day and night**
  [deɪ ænd naɪt] 日以繼夜
- **in** [ɪn] 在……期間
  （表時間）
- **finish** [ˋfɪn.ɪʃ] 完成
- **pour** [pɔ:r]
  （雨）傾盆而下
- **bright** [braɪt] 明亮的
- **lightning** [ˋlaɪt.nɪŋ]
  閃電；雷光
- **loud** [laʊd] 大聲的
- **thunder** [ˋθʌn.də] 雷鳴
- **temple** [ˋtem.pl̩] 寺廟

---

p. 36

但宙斯仍不滿意，
他說：
「波賽墩，我需要你的幫忙。
你是水域之神，
運用你偉大的力量，
讓洪水淹沒大地，寸土不留！」
波賽墩於是舉矛擊水，
掀起巨浪。
霎時，群山也被吞噬了。

- **satisfied** [ˋsæt̬.ɪs.faɪd]
  滿足
- **mighty** [ˋmaɪ.t̬i]
  威力強大的
- **dry** [draɪ] 乾的
- **hit** [hɪt] 擊中
- **spear** [spɪr] 矛
- **wave** [weɪv] 浪；波浪
- **came up** [keɪm ʌp]
  升上來
  （come up的過去式）

p. 37

但在船上的鐸卡連和皮雅，安然無恙。
動物和食物，也都毫無損傷。
暴風雨連續了九天九夜，
鐸卡連和皮雅感到恐慌，
生怕暴風雨會永遠繼續下去。
他們向宙斯祈禱，
請求宙斯停止暴風雨。

- **storm** [stɔːrm] 風暴
- **continue** [kən`tɪn.juː] 持續著
- **scared** [skerd] 驚恐的；恐懼的
- **pray** [preɪ] 祈禱

p. 38

宙斯聽到了他們的祈求，
他知道鐸卡連和皮雅都是善民，
也確定了其他的人類都已經被消滅。
大地一片死寂。
宙斯憐憫鐸卡連和皮雅，
便停止了暴風雨。

- **prayer** [prer] 祈求的事物
- **knew** [nuː] 知曉；知情（know 的過去式）
- **alive** [ə`laɪv] 活著的
- **else** [els] 其他的；別的
- **dead** [ded] 死寂的；枯萎的

p. 39

天空終於放晴，
只是望眼都是汪洋。
鐸卡連的船在水上漂流多日，
鐸卡連和妻子天天都向宙斯祈禱。
終於，大水開始消退。
大船最後停在了巴拿撒斯山的山頂。
鐸卡連和妻子兩人將船門打開，

- **at last** [æt læst] 最後；終於
- **everywhere** [`ev.ri.wer] 到處
- **for days** [fə deɪs] 持續了幾天
- **float** [floʊt] 漂流
- **go down** [goʊ daʊn] 消退
- **mount** [maʊnt] 山脈

把動物都放了出來。

- **let** [lɛt] 使；讓

p. 40

(Did you know)

巴拿撒斯山

巴拿撒斯山位於狄菲市鎮旁，
阿波羅曾在這裡殺過一隻可怕的巨蟒。
古希臘人在這裡舉行運動會，
以紀念阿波羅的殺蟒事蹟。
在市鎮附近，
有一座遠近馳名的神殿，
是為阿波羅神所建造的。

- **town** [taʊn] 市鎮；城鎮
- **scary** [ˋskɛr.i]
  嚇人的；可怕的
- **huge** [hjuːdʒ] 巨大的
- **snake** [sneɪk] 蟒；蛇
- **special** [ˋspɛʃəl]
  與眾不同的
- **event** [ɪˋvɛnt] 事件
- **remember** [rɪˋmɛm.bɚ]
  記得
- **famous** [ˋfei.məs]
  出名的；著名的

p. 41

鐸卡連和皮雅來到神殿，
神殿因洪水而損壞嚴重。
他們點起火，開始祈禱。
首先，他們感謝眾神之王宙斯，
接著，鐸卡連說：
「世界只剩下我們兩人，
應該要有更多人類的。
宙斯，請幫助我們吧。」

- **condition** [kənˋdɪʃ.ən]
  情況；狀態
- **lit** [lɪt] 點燃
  （light的過去式）
- **thank** [θæŋk] 感謝
- **alone** [əˋləʊn]
  單獨的；僅僅

p. 42

宙斯又聽到了鐸卡連的禱告。
他說：
「離開寺廟，等你走出門時，
把你母親的骨頭，丟在地上！」
皮雅很震驚，說道：
「我不能把我母親的骨頭丟在地上呀！」

- **leave** [li:v] 離開
- **outside** [ˌaʊtˋsaɪd]
  在外頭
- **get outside** [get ˌaʊtˋsaɪd]
  到室外
- **throw** [θroʊ] 扔
- **bone** [boʊn] 骨頭
- **ground** [graʊnd]
  地面；地上
- **shocked** [ʃɑ:kt] 衝撞

p. 43

鐸卡連和皮雅走出神殿。
「我們不能這樣做！」皮雅說。
鐸卡連對此思考良久。
突然，他說：
「我明白宙斯的意思了！
大地是人類之母，
石頭一如大地之骨，
我們就把石頭丟在地上吧！」

- **for a long time**
  [fə eɪ lɑ:ŋ taɪm]
  持續一段很長的時間
- **meant** [ment]
  表示……的意思
  （mean的過去式）
- **rock** [rɑ:k] 石頭

p. 44

他們於是撿了許多石頭，

然後沿著神殿，

丟下了幾百顆的石頭。

他們回頭一看，驚訝不已。

- **pick up** [pɪk ʌp]
  拾起；撿起
- **walk around**
  [wɑːk əˋraʊnd]
  沿著……的周圍走
- **hundred** [ˋhʌn.drəd] 百
- **hundreds of**
  [ˋhʌn.drəds aːv]
  數以百計的
- **surprised** [səˋpraɪzd]
  驚訝

---

 p. 45

石頭竟慢慢變軟，

然後開始動了起來，

開始現出人形。

一顆顆的石頭變成了人類。

鐸卡連丟的石頭變成男人，

皮雅丟的石頭變成女人。

新的人類，不如舊人類，

但他們努力向上，辛勤工作。

- **slowly** [ˋsloʊ.li]
  緩慢地
- **soft** [sɑːft] 軟的
- **wiggle** [ˋwɪg.l] 扭曲
- **shook** [ʃʊk]
  搖動
  （shake的過去式）
- **change into**
  [tʃeɪndʒ ˋɪn.tuː] 變成
- **before** [bɪˋfɔːr] 從前
- **well** [wel]
  好地；令人滿意地

p. 46

宙斯從奧林帕斯山上往下看。
新的人類努力不懈,相互幫助,
於是,
真理與誠實又回到了人間。

- **each other** [i:tʃ `ʌðɚ]
  互相;彼此
- **came back** [keɪm bæk]
  回來;恢復到原來的樣
  子(come back的過去
  式)

---

p. 47

此外,新的人類對眾神祈禱,
這深得宙斯的心,
宙斯便再也不製造洪水消滅世界了。

- **flood** [flʌd] 使淹沒

---

 p. 48

(Did you know)

諾亞方舟

在聖經中,
也有類似的大洪水故事。
在聖經故事裡,
上帝看到世上有許多惡人,
因此決定用大洪水淹沒世界。

但上帝想起了諾亞。
諾亞一家人,是唯一的善人。

- **the Bible** [ðə `baɪ.bl̩]
  聖經
- **similar to** [`sɪm.ə.lɚ tə]
  相似於……
- **saw** [sɑ:] 看見
  (see的過去式)
- **decide** [dɪ`saɪd] 決定
- **cover** [`kʌv.ɚ] 覆蓋
- **remember** [rɪ`membɚ]
  記起;記得
- **huge** [hju:dʒ] 巨大的

所以在大洪水來臨的七天前，
上帝要諾亞建造巨船，
這艘船就叫做「諾亞方舟」。
諾亞為家人建造方舟，
並將各種動物帶上船，
動物各一公一母。
大雨一連下了四十天，
但方舟內的諾亞一家人和動物，
皆安全度過。

閱讀測驗

Part 1

p. 51 ~ p. 52

Part 1普羅米修斯和潘朵拉

※ **閱讀下列問題並選出最適當的答案。**

1. 哪一位是普羅米修斯的愚昧胞弟？
   (A) 伊比米修斯　　　(B) 波賽墩
   (C) 宙斯　　　　　　(D) 赫發斯特斯　　　答案 (A)

2. 誰盜取了火？
   (A) 伊比米修斯　　　(B) 普羅米修斯
   (C) 人類　　　　　　(D) 赫發斯特斯　　　答案 (B)

3. 普羅米修斯是＿＿＿＿＿＿＿＿＿＿？
   (A) 神明　　　　　　(B) 人類
   (C) 泰坦神　　　　　(D) 動物

   答案 (C)

4. 誰教潘朵拉夫說謊？

    (A) 赫丘力　　　　　(B) 雅典那

    (C) 荷米斯　　　　　(D) 阿波羅　　　　　答案 (C)

5. 在空格內填入正確答案。

    動物的眼睛往下看，對著_____。　　答案 earth

    人類的眼睛往上看，對著_____。　　答案 stars

6. 誰釋放了普羅米修斯？

    (A) 伊比米修斯　　(B)赫拉　　　　　答案 (D)

    (C) 宙斯　　　　　(D) 赫丘力

7. 普羅米修斯用了什麼東西與水混合後製造出人類？

    (A) 空氣　　　　　(B) 土地

    (C) 光　　　　　　(D) 鹽巴　　　　　答案 (B)

8. 下面哪一個不是從潘朵拉的盒子裡跑出來的？

  (A) 戰爭　　　　　　(B) 疾病

  (C) 希望　　　　　　(D) 打鬥

答案 (C)

p. 53 ~ p. 54

※閱讀下列問題並選出最適當的答案。

1. 誰是鐸卡連？
   (A) 伊比米修斯之子 (B) 普羅米修斯之子
   (C) 赫拉之子　　　　(D) 皮雅之子

   答案 (B)

2. 誰是鐸卡連之妻？
   (A) 潘朵拉　　　　　(B) 雅典那
   (C) 赫拉　　　　　　(D) 皮雅

   答案 (D)

3. 誰幫助宙斯淹沒大地？
   (A) 鐸卡連　　　　　(B) 波賽墩
   (C) 海地士　　　　　(D) 阿波羅

   答案 (B)

4. 大雨連下了幾天？
   (A) 七天　　　　　(B) 八天
   (C) 九天　　　　　(D) 十天
   答案 (C)

5. 宙斯所說的「母親的骨頭」是指什麼？
   (A) 空氣　　　　　(B) 土地
   (C) 水　　　　　　(D) 石頭
   答案 (D)

6. 在空格內填入正確答案。

   鐸卡連的石頭變成了＿＿＿＿＿。
   答案 men

   皮雅的石頭變成了＿＿＿＿＿。
   答案 women

7. 什麼不會讓宙斯發怒？
   (A) 人類長期戰爭，死傷無數。
   (B) 人人都說謊。
   (C) 人類破壞大地。
   (D) 人類向神祈禱。
   答案 (D)

26

Greek Roman Myths 故事原著作者 *Thomas Bulfinch*

Without a knowledge of mythology much of the elegant literature of our own language cannot be understood and appreciated.

　　缺少了神話知識，就無法了解和透徹語言的文學之美。

　　　　　　　　　　　　　　　　　　—Thomas Bulfinch

　　Thomas Bulfinch（1796-1867），出生於美國麻薩諸塞州的Newton，隨後全家移居波士頓，父親爲知名的建築師Charles Bulfinch。他在求學時期，曾就讀過一些優異的名校，並於1814年畢業於哈佛。

　　畢業後，執過教鞭，爾後從商，但經濟狀況一直未能穩定。1837年，在銀行擔任一般職員，以此爲終身職業。後來開始進一步鑽研古典文學，成爲業餘作家，一生未婚。

　　1855年，時值59歲，出版了奠立其作家地位的名作*The Age of Fables*，書中蒐集希臘羅馬神話，廣受歡迎。此書後來與日後出版的 *The Age of Chivalry*（1858）和 *Legends of Charlemagne*（1863），合集更名爲 *Bulfinch's Mythology*。

　　本系列書系，即改編自 *The Age of Fable*。Bulfinch 著寫本書時，特地以成年大眾爲對象，以將古典文學引介給一般大眾。*The Age of Fable* 堪稱十九世紀的羅馬神話故事的重要代表著作，其中有很多故事來源，來自Bulfinch自己對奧維德（Ovid）的《變形記》（*Metamorphoses*）的翻譯。

■Bulfinch的著作

1. Hebrew Lyrical History.
2. The Age of Fable: Or Stories of Gods and Heroes.
3. The Age of Chivalry.
4. The Boy Inventor: A Memoir of Matthew Edwards, Mathematical-Instrument Maker.
5. Legends of Charlemagne.
6. Poetry of the Age of Fable.
7. Shakespeare Adapted for Reading Classes.
8. Oregon and Eldorado.
9. Bulfinch's Mythology: Age of Fable, Age of Chivalry, Legends of Charlemagne.